Love That Never Completed

"Incomplete love of a boy"

AMAN GUPTA

First Published in December 2020

ISBN: 978-93-5427-150-2

BLUEROSE PUBLISHERS

www.bluerosepublishers.com

info@bluerosepublishers.com

+91 8882 898 898

Cover Design:

Joel Pariat

Typographic Design:

Ayushi Garg

Distributed by: BlueRose, Amazon, Flipkart, Shopclues

Hum mohabbat karne se pehle, shartein nahi rakhte

Ki jab tak hum apne partner se mohabbat karenge, usko bhi karni hogi.

Nahi rakhte na?

Fir uske chale jane ke baad afsos kyun karna?

Har ishq ka ek waqt hota hai, wo hamara waqt nahi tha.

Par iska matlab ye nahi vo ishq nahi tha,

Har ishq mukaml ho ye zaruri nahi.

Ye book uss ladki ke liye hai, jisne mujhse bepanha Mohabbat ki,

Usne har vo koshish ki, jisse wo meri ho sake.

Bus abhi khuda razi nahi hai,

Jab khuda razi hoga, toh duniya ki har cheez meri hogi.

Amen!

About Us

Hum dono nursery class se ek saath padhte thei. Na hum dost the na hee ajnabi. Na hee kabhi ek doosre se baat karte thei. Bas wo mujhe jaanti thi aur main usey. Hum dono ke beech Rishta tha toh vo tha sirf classmates or schoolmates ka. Kabhi uske liye koi feeling ayi hee nahi. Par fir ek waqt aya jab sab badal gaya.

Aur ye kahaani shuru hui...!

3 November 2012

It was her birthday. I was going to talk to her for the first time today. Although I had her mobile number already, I had never bothered calling or messaging her any time before.

I picked up my phone and dropped her a message saying, 'Happy birthday.' As expected, her response was, 'Who are you?' and I replied promptly with a 'Please thank me first.' 'Thank you. Now tell me who exactly are you?' she replied. I told her, 'I will tell you after coming back from the school, okay bye, and Happy Birthday once again!' There was no message exchange after that.

Every day I would go to the school, and she would appear before me, but today I couldn't look into her eyes. I was feeling different in an indescribable way.

Even in a crowd of 100 girls, I had my eyes only for her. Her smile, her eyes, and her every movement looked unusual.

I was thinking of her the entire time in the school. I would peek a glance at her whenever I could. She looked radiantly different today.

In the evening, she messaged me to ask, 'Now tell me your name?' 'Aman Gupta,' I told her the truth. She couldn't believe it was me, claiming she knew Aman Gupta very well. It was then I decided to tell her our childhood stories, which she had forgotten entirely. She never responded after that.

The next day at school, a friend of hers approached me and asked, 'Aman, did you message Kanika yesterday?'

I replied, 'I did. Why, what happened?' She told me that Kanika was very stressed, and that I should not message or annoy her again. I questioned her why shouldn't I, and that I will. And then, I left for my class.

Some moments later, one of the teachers came looking for me. She asked me to step out of the class and took me to her office telling me that what I was doing was wrong, and I should stop messaging the girl. And if I don't stop, she will tell the professor about it. I told her to go ahead and do it and she did.

The professor was someone I respected a lot. He approached me and asked the same thing – that I should stop messaging her. I told him that I would.

And so, I didn't message her after that. A few days later, on 11 November, it was a leave due to the Diwali festival, and I sent her a 'Happy Diwali to you and your family' greeting. She replied, 'Same to you.' I assumed she had no problem talking to me and sent her another message asking, 'How are you?' There was no reply. I tried calling her, but she cut the call. The next day, I sent her another greeting, 'Happy Govardhan,' and again, no response. I tried to call her again and again, and she kept rejecting them. And then, she put my number on the block list. The next day, I started calling her number right from the morning trying to reach her, but she got stressed and told her family. Her father came to my home and told my family everything.

Because of what her father told, it caused a lot of trouble for me. I was angry at her, but I could not understand her perspective in all my rage. Every time I would see her at school, I had these killing instincts. But eventually, I started liking her. I would stare at her, ask her friends about her, and only talk things about her. Daringly, I asked her friend to help me talk to her just once.

And thanks to her friend, she came to meet me. She told me to state my intentions, and I asked if I was still troubling her. She agreed that I wasn't. I told her that I wasn't so bad that she couldn't talk to me. She asked me to understand that she wasn't comfortable talking to me. Still, I insisted, 'I will wait for your message today.' Her response was, 'Sure, wait. Because I won't message.'

But guess what, she did message me. 'Hi, this is Kanika. What do you want? Why don't you understand that you should focus on your studies?' And she kept on repeating that. She said, 'Aman, we don't have a future together.' And that was the only reason that she did not want to talk to me. I insisted that we could still be friends, and she said she would need some time to think about it, as she doesn't just randomly pick her friends.

I repeatedly told her that all I wanted was to be a stranger no longer. Again, she said that she will give it a thought, and that for now, being schoolmates should be good enough. But I was stubborn, and she eventually relented to my request and said that we are just friends and no more. After that, we would talk a lot daily.

The school was all set to prepare for the annual day celebrations. She was a fantastic singer as well as a dancer. She was to represent about five different programs in a lead role. I participated too just to be around her. Then one day, I got a call from a teacher, and she confirmed if I had brought my phone to school. She asked me to leave my phone and collect it later. The girls needed it to play songs for dance practice because the school audio system wasn't functioning. I deleted all my text exchanges with Kanika and gave the phone to another girl from my class and told her to protect it with her life and not give it to anyone no matter what. She agreed to it.

In the evening, she returned my phone and asked what was going on between Kanika and me. I denied there was anything, but she said that there is something and left giggling. Since I had deleted all the messages, I could not understand this behaviour of hers. Shortly after, Kanika messaged and thanked me for helping, that if I hadn't given my phone, the practice would have been cut short. She asked me if I wasn't scared to get my phone to school, and what if someone caught me? And then, she started explaining to me the consequences and warned me not to get the phone to school, as it was just a matter of six hours without it.

A few moments later, she enquired if she could ask me something without me judging her. I said yes, so she told me that she had checked my phone and apologised for doing so. The phone was with Deeksha, and she had asked whose phone it was. When she found out it was mine, she couldn't resist taking it and looking at all the messages and photos on it. And she apologised again. I said that it was because of what she did that Deeksha found out something was going on between her and me. Shocked, she said that I should deny all such claims about us, and I agreed to talk to Deeksha the next day about it. And then she left saying goodbye.

The next day at school, I took Deeksha aside and asked her why she had doubts about Kanika and me. She reiterated the story about Kanika taking my phone. I told Deeksha that it wasn't a big deal, and she should stop fussing about it. But she told me that only when Kanika found out it was my phone, she started checking all my messages, my Facebook, and the photos. I denied it again saying that she was overthinking. She agreed and mocked me saying that things like flirting or being involved with girls isn't something that I do, and she would have looked at my phone casually.

I felt happily positive wondering why she would check my phone, as she thinks of me as just a friend. I would keep smiling at this thought. After this, I gave my phone to her multiple times, and every time she would check something on it. And then, the annual function ended, and we would keep talking like that.

On the 1st of February, my phone got caught in school, and I forgot to clear all the chats. One of the teachers read our conversation and told my sister that Kanika and I talk regularly. When I tried to get my phone, the teacher told me that she would give it only to my parents and that I should stay away from the girl. She also said that I wasn't letting her study and was ruining her life. I told the teacher that we were just friends. She said that the chats didn't look anything like 'just friends,' and if anyone else would agree to that, she would give the phone to me right then and there. But she kept it anyway. Kanika feared that the teacher would tell her parents, so to avoid that from happening, she told them everything.

On the 2nd of February, her father came to my home and told everyone what happened. My dad was furious at me and told me to ensure this would not happen again.

After that, I tried my best to meet her, but she wouldn't meet me. She would not talk to me either. I had started feeling something for her by then, and maybe it was love. I would go to the school only to look at her and would talk only about her. I would ask her friends about her all the time. Before she left for home, I would drop by the bus stand to have a peek at her, or else I would have to wait a whole day to see her again. I would ask her to meet and talk to me, but she would refuse. I would go to the school everyday thinking to meet her any way possible, and she would avoid me every time.

On the occasion of Holi, I got a message from her, 'How are you, Aman?' 'I'm fine. How about you?' I replied. She told me that she wished all her friends, so she decided to message me too. I asked if she still considered me only a friend, but she got agitated and asked if she should talk to me. She asked if I have a problem whether she talks to me or not. I told her it was nothing like that. We talked for quite some time after that.

Finally, I told her, 'I love you, Kanika!' She responded, 'Forget about me, Aman. We don't have a future together, as our parents won't agree to it.' I asked if we would still be friends, and she said that we were friends before. That one mistake of mine caused her to be in trouble at her home, and she needed to ask permission even for small things like using Facebook. I told her that I would never get my phone to school again, as she mattered more than a phone. She warned me that if something wrong happens again and people find out about us, I won't be able to see her, forget talking to her. So, she agreed we were friends again, but she would talk to me when she had the time, and I shouldn't initiate the conversation. I would neither message nor call her, and we were nothing more than friends.

I asked her if she loved me, and she responded, 'I don't know.' I asked her to respond with a yes or no, to which she said, 'I will tell you when it's the right time.' I demanded a date for the response, and she said that she would answer me once the class 12 exams were over. But I persisted with her for a specific date, and I promised I wouldn't ask her anything until then. She said, 'After the exams on 1 April 2014.' I asked her for the next day. She promised she wasn't trying to play an 'April Fools' joke on me, and so she agreed for the 2nd of April. I asked her again that I would need a confirm answer. But she was curious if I would wait till then, and what if she said no? I told her that I would agree to whatever she would decide.

After that, we would casually talk, sometimes on a message or on Facebook, and a couple of times on call. We had started sharing a lot of things. She started relying on me more about her problems, and I would do the same. We were getting closer to each other, but she would always keep reminding me that her answer will be in due time, and we are friends, and that should be enough.

My life was going smooth, and I had understood enough by then that she started loving me too but would only say no and not feel that way. We would meet in school during lunchtime, and I would keep staring at her while she blabbered, and then she would ask me if she talked too much. I would shake my head and say no, and she would smile and call me mad and then walk away. Things were going good, her studies weren't being disturbed, and our friendship was going strong.

Once summer vacations started, she told me that she would message if she could find the time, but asked me not to do it as it would start another drama at home.

On 7 June 2013, she called me at 5:04 am and asked me to talk to her. I was so sleepy that I couldn't open my eyes properly, and I did not see who was calling.

Once I heard the voice, I woke up for real and realised she was calling. I asked how she was able to talk, was no one home? And she told me that she was at her grandparents' house, so she can talk.

I got ready quickly and went outside to talk to her, which we did for about three hours that day. She was in the park outside her grandparents' house and was telling me everything about her past and present. In between talking about our future, I told her, 'I love you' so many times, but every time she would say something like, 'Try to understand, Aman. We don't have a future together' or 'Will give a reply after 12th.' Before dropping the call, she asked me to wait till 3 pm to talk again and requested me not to call or message till then. I agreed and said that I would wait for her, and we both went inside our homes.

Around 10 am, she called, but I couldn't pick up, and I noticed the missed call an hour later. I didn't call back because I promised I wouldn't. At 3 pm, I got a call. I picked up, but it was a male voice, so I cut the call immediately. And there were no further calls. I waited till the evening for her to call, but nothing. I couldn't sleep thinking she would call anytime, and I would miss it. She didn't call the entire day, and I couldn't muster up the courage to call as she would get mad and would fight with me.

Fourteen days passed as I waited patiently. One of my friends called me and asked to meet me. I went to meet him. He said his girlfriend had told him that Kanika's parents found out that Kanika and I were talking again, and we both were so busy talking that she did not notice her parents continuously calling her. When she returned home, they checked her call logs and it showed my number there. And as a consequence, she would never talk to me or meet me.

She even had him convey a message that I shouldn't try to meet her or try to contact her. If I loved her, I would understand and wouldn't force her to meet me and would promise it to myself in her name. Hearing all that, I couldn't stop myself from crying. Not being able to talk to her was difficult, but I realised that she knew how much she meant to me, and how much the promise mattered to me.

School resumed on 26 June. I was the first to reach school in the morning, and when I saw her there, I had tears in my eyes. I thought about going and talking to her, but I remembered my promise. That promise mattered more to me than her, so I controlled myself. But I lost that control after a few days, and I just wanted to listen her voice. I wanted her to talk to me once, so I asked a friend to help me contact her. The condition was that I would never appear in front of her again if she talked to me once. My friend brought her to me, and she asked me what I wanted. I forgot everything when I saw her and couldn't tell her anything. The only thing I could say was that this was all wrong, and that what was the point of the promise of not talking or meeting if she didn't believe in it. I asked her to give me an explanation. She asked me to understand her problem, and asked if I didn't want to see her even at school. She told me that if I liked her, I shouldn't talk to her or ask to meet her and try my best to forget her, again repeating that we had no future together. She told me how her mother made her promise that she wouldn't talk to me, and then she left.

I was dumbfounded and couldn't move from the spot. She just came and left, asking me to forget her. I thought if she were happy staying away from me, I would respect her wish. And thus, I decided not to even appear in front of her, forget about looking at her.

I stopped going to school, and if I did, it was always late and would always stay inside my classroom. Kanika would keep asking my friends about my whereabouts and why wasn't I coming to school and if I was doing well. I was trying my best to stop myself from meeting her. I would never meet her directly, and I thought I shouldn't make her worry, but it was a different feeling trying to peek at her from afar, and it was exciting to do that.

It had been a month since I last talked to her, and then I couldn't resist anymore. On the 4th of August, there was a school program going on, and all the students were attending it. There was no one on the top floor except a friend of mine and me. During this time, Kanika entered her class, and I decided I would finally ask her if she liked me, as she would keep asking about me but still wouldn't do anything more. And if she didn't bother, then I shouldn't either.

I went outside her classroom and called her. She came and asked me what I wanted. I asked her to clearly state her intentions, to which she responded that she didn't want anything, and asked why I was asking her about her intentions. I enquired about her curiosity to ask my friends about me, and she said that it is her decision to ask about whoever she wants, and it shouldn't bother me. I pleaded with her to tell me what she meant. I said that I love her. I stayed away from her but couldn't anymore. I told her that I remembered the promise I made that kept me away from her, but now I wanted to meet her and talk to her every day, even for two minutes. All she replied was, 'Hmm.' I asked her to say yes or no, if she loved me. She tried to reiterate that we had no future together, but I completed it before she could finish it. I asked her what we can do about it and told her that we should try to be happy together as much as we can be, at least for that time. She agreed.

Then, I said, 'I love you' and asked her if she did too. She said yes, and hearing that, I couldn't contain my happiness. Then, we talked about everything and left for home afterwards.

The next day we met for five mins, but it felt like an eternity. I was happy that we were talking even for a short time. But eventually, she started ignoring me, and wouldn't respond to me calling her to meet. She would avoid looking at me and so much more.

On the 25th of August, I asked her to meet me. I gave her the context of the promise that I made her before.

I asked her what was wrong and if it was something I did. She said that nothing was wrong, it was just that we couldn't continue our relationship anymore, and she asked me to forget her again if I loved her. I didn't say anything and left smiling.

I thought a lot about what to do after that, and then I concluded that even if I loved her, it doesn't necessarily mean that she loves me back. I wrote her a 16-page letter saying everything I felt about her, like how important she was to me and why. It felt more like an essay than a letter. At the end of it, I wrote, 'Sure, it's fine that you may not love me; I do love you and will continue doing so. I will not say it is for a lifetime, but I will love you more than life itself till the time I do. I will never let you feel that there is a guy called Aman around you, you will never have any troubles because of me, and I will never come around you. So, goodbye and take care. I love you so much.'

A friend sent this letter on my behalf on the 4th of September. During lunch, the friend told me that Kanika wants to meet me after lunch. I didn't feel like meeting her but thought I should do it for the last time. I approached her, and she asked me, 'What is this?' and I said, 'It's a letter.' She said that she knows what it is, but asked me the meaning of all of this. I said, 'Whatever I have written is the truth. If you are happy being away from me, then so be it.' She said nothing, and I just kept looking at her. After a long silence, I said, 'Goodbye and take care. We may not meet again.'

As I tried to get up, she grabbed my hand and said that this wasn't done as she called me to meet. She asked me to sit, and I said there was no point. And then she said, 'I love you, Aman. I love you so much. I did not know I matter so much to you. You remember every single date and memories of ours. If you had remembered the study books so much, you would have topped the school.' While I was thrilled, I told her that there is no point since she will just yet again say that we have no future together.

Angrily, but lovingly, she said that she doesn't care about the future anymore and wants to be together with me, and she can't live without me anymore. She told me that she loves me so much, and she would never leave me again, nor would she let me go.

It was that moment that I would cherish for years to come. I thought I was dreaming and asked Kanika to pinch me. She said that she was telling the truth about loving me, and she can do anything to make me believe it. I was stupefied listening to her because what I wanted to have for so long, I finally had. And that too, when I was ready to sacrifice everything for her happiness. I told her I believed her. We held hands and looked at each other for a long time after that. I wanted to stop time then and there. I yearn to relive those moments again.

The next day it was 5 September, Teachers' Day celebrations. We went to school and spent all day together, and I can never forget that day. I shared all my feelings, and she respected them. We decided not to meet at school or call each other, and when we would want to talk, it would be done through a letter exchange. We would pour our heart out into that letter, and that feeling was quite exciting, waiting to receive one from each other. It was nostalgic to write letters even in an era of technology. We would barely meet in school for five or ten minutes, and we would occasionally fight, at least once every 15 days, initiated by either one of us. The fights were for stupid reasons, but it was those fights that brought us together, and we started to understand each other.

It was challenging to make it up to her once she got angry, but trying to make her smile was worth it. She would get upset the same way a child would. Even if the mistake were hers, I would always be the one apologising. How September and October had passed quickly, we didn't even notice, as whenever we met, we would live in the moment.

Her birthday was approaching – 3 November. I asked her if there was anything special that she wanted. She said that moments like these wouldn't come again, so she would need to think about it. After three days, she made a demand, and I got it for her. I was very excited to give it to her, but I couldn't give it to her on her birthday. It was because the 3rd of November was Diwali, and school vacations started from the 2nd.

On the 1st, it was a teachers' cricket match, so everyone in the school was watching it, while I had my eyes only for her. I made a plan to wish her physically, and I would give the gift then, hoping she would be pleased about it. I asked a classmate of hers to help, saying that I wanted to meet her. She told Kanika, but she did not come to meet. I asked another friend to help, but to no avail, she refused again as she wanted to watch the cricket match. I tried asking to meet her at least five to six times, and every time she had the same reaction. I waited for her for two hours standing at a single spot, where she could see me, but she didn't take a single glance at me. I lost my cool that day. Her best friend approached me, and in my frustration, I said a lot of bad things about her, like what Kanika thinks of herself, and that I keep girls like her in my pockets. I asked her to go and tell her not to show her face to me again. She conveyed my message to Kanika, and I saw her crying and running to her class. Watching her cry, I felt guilty about my actions, and I followed her. Her friend was waiting outside her class, and as I tried to enter, she stopped me. I asked her to mind her own business as I entered. Kanika was there, crying non-stop. I apologised consistently and tried to make up, but she wouldn't listen to anything. I held her and forcibly made her slap me, but in vain. She said that if girls like her are in my pocket, then she shouldn't matter.

During this time, the match ended, and as everyone returned to their respective classrooms, the school bell rang. She left the class before I could wish her. I cried a lot that day because I made her cry while I longed to see and make her smile. On the 2nd of November, all I could think of was trying to find a way to wish her the first. She did not have a phone anymore, and she had stopped calling me. Since it was Diwali eve on the 3rd, I couldn't find a way to step outside my home. It was pointless trying during the night time. Still, I whispered to the wind and wished her a happy birthday, going outside her home at midnight. She wasn't there, but I did it to please my heavy heart. We celebrated her birthday in the evening with all our friends. A friend's brother's daughter cut her birthday cake, and the little girl was delighted to do the deed. Looking at that girl's smile, I could see Kanika's image in her.

After that, I would wait every day for her message, thinking she would understand why I was so angry that day, but she never did. When the school opened on 7 November after vacation, I asked her to meet during lunch break. I apologised as soon as she came. She said with an attitude that she wouldn't accept the apology, as she has forgiven me many times, and every time I would make some new mistake again. If girls like her are in my pocket, I should keep them and leave her alone. She said that she was sorry and that I shouldn't be, and that we should go our separate ways.

I told her that I had been waiting for her for so long. I had asked so many girls to fetch her. And because she didn't, I got mad and said those horrible things out of frustration. I apologised again.

After that, she calmed down a bit and said that I am the one who always makes a mistake and apologises every time. But this time, there will be no apology. I asked her to give me any punishment, and I will take it if she forgives me. I held my ears and crouched on my knees and said sorry. And then, she smiled and said that she forgave me.

Then, I wished her belated birthday greetings and gave her the gift I got for her. I told her how we celebrated her birthday, and then she thanked me and told me that she loved me a lot.

And then, everything was back to normal again. We would meet every day for five minutes and exchange letters as usual. November passed just like that, and our pre-board examinations started. I asked her to meet one day, but she did not come. I thought she must have been busy, so I didn't pay much heed to it.

But then, for four days, she ignored me. I asked her friend if she knew anything about it. The friend said that she won't say anything except that Kanika would not meet me again ever. I was so frustrated because I hadn't done anything wrong, and I was wondering what made her upset. I asked her friend to arrange a meeting anyway so I can at least understand what was happening. The friend reiterated that Kanika would not come to meet me, and I told her to at least try since I wanted to meet her.

The friend went to fetch her, but she refused to come. And the friend came to me and reaffirmed everything she said about Kanika. I asked her if she knew anything, and she said that it was because I commented, 'You are so beautiful. I wish I could be by your side,' on Richa's posts. Richa was the girlfriend of a friend of mine and had already completed school. The friend told me that Ms Reenu, one of the teachers, had told Kanika that I loved Richa and not her, and I was only passing my time and backstabbing her. I smiled and asked her friend just to tell her that I had promised her something and that all I ask for is one meeting. And then, she came to meet me and asked me why I wanted to meet her.

I asked her if she thought I was capable of the accusations made against me. She said that it wasn't about being capable or not, she had herself seen the comments on her profile and anyone could infer that I loved Richa. I reassured her and told her that there was nothing like that, and I would give any proof she needs that I had my eyes only for her. I treated Richa like my sister and made some jokes with her, as she was my friend Ayush's girlfriend, and even Richa knew it. Putting that aside, I have her if there were signs of me fooling around with her. Even if we added up all the time we spent together, it was barely 32 hours in all, which included meeting face-to-face or talking on the phone ever since we had been together.

She asked me what was the meaning of that comment, and I told her that she could think whatever she wants, and I will give a reasonable explanation in my way – saying that, I left.

I collected all the letters she wrote to me and gave them all to her friend. I asked the friend to convey the message that I no longer had anything of hers, just the memories which she cannot take away from me. Then I went to my classroom and cut off my wrist. A friend of mine came and slapped me, cleaning the blood with a handkerchief. I took my bag and walked away from the room.

Meanwhile, Kanika heard what I had done, and she waited for me at the stairs. She asked me to listen to her, and before she could continue, I put my hands together, pleaded, and walked downstairs. She followed me and tried calling me to stop and listen to her, but I just ignored her and walked away. In the evening, Ms Meenu called me and asked my whereabouts. I told her that I was going to my tuition, but she asked me to come to meet her instead. I said that I would meet her in school the next day, as the tuition was essential, and I needed to go. Agitated, she asked me to come and forget all about my studies.

So, I went to her place and found Kanika waiting for me there. Ms Meenu said that I was being over-smart and flying high and that she will call my parents and tell them about how I cut my wrist. I asked her if she knew their number, or I should provide it. And then, Kanika asked me why I did what I did, and why I couldn't talk to her calmly. I told her that I would do whatever I want, and she shouldn't bother about it.

Ms Meenu said that my comments were obviously inappropriate, and anyone would think so. I said that I do not care what anyone thought about it, as I know I didn't do anything wrong, and that Kanika should stay happy with her life, and let me be in mine – saying that, I left the place.

The next day in school, I called Kanika to meet and apologise to her, but she did not come at first. As she was going for her class, I took her aside and said that I was sorry and that I would not make such comments again, and it was the truth that I would joke with Richa, and she can confirm it with her.
She said that as I said the day before that she should be happy with her life and let me be happy in mine, so

I should do that. We should not be concerned with each other anymore, and I shouldn't try to stop her from leaving. I started crying as I apologised and sat down on the floor, pleading to her to stop, or I would die. I tried my best to stop her, but she didn't and left crying. I thought I was so hapless since I made her cry again, and I wondered why I said such horrible things to her when she was my whole world.

I took my bike out and went straight to the highway. My friends followed me and noticed me shivering in the cold. I kept on crying, and my friends asked me to go home and think calmly. They said that both of us would fight regularly, and things would settle down again shortly. I left and decided to punish myself in some way.

After some time, a friend of mine called me and said that Kanika was asking for me to ensure I hadn't done anything stupid. My friend asked if I did something, and I told him that some punishment was due, that her name had seven letters in it and after seven days she will forgive him.

Every day since then, I would write an alphabetic letter from her name on my hands using a blade. My friends tried their best to stop me and said that she would feel terrible about it and might not forgive me. I told them that even if she didn't, I was ready to take that gamble as I was being punished for my deeds. One of my friends got mad at Kanika and told her everything I was doing and how I had lost my mind and that she was the reason for my condition. Since she didn't know what was happening before, she asked to meet me when she found out.

I had stopped going to school by then, so my friend called me and asked me to come to the school urgently, lying that he had fought with someone. He knew if he told me that Kanika was the one asking for me, I wouldn't come. So I went to school, and my friend apologised and told me the truth that it was Kanika who had called me, and that I should meet her once for his sake. I told him that I didn't want to, but he still insisted, so I agreed and went to meet her.

She asked me what kind of madness this was, what if something had happened to me, and what would she feel and do about it. I told her that nothing had happened and that nothing would happen to her, and I was just punishing myself. She asked me to forget everything and apologised. I told her not to, as I should be the one apologising. Then, she told me that it was her fault that she had doubts about me. I told her that it was still my mistake, and I shouldn't have said the things I did that day. And thus, she said that we should forgive each other and promise that we wouldn't fight again. I told her I loved her, and as a force of habit, she said, 'I know, tell me something new.' And then she left. After all that, she would not fight anymore. Sometimes we would get a little mad at each other, but that was it.

Our farewell arrived shortly, and we were all excited about it. I felt this uneasiness in the pit of my stomach that everyone was going to part ways soon. On the day of the farewell, I asked her to meet me inside a classroom. She did and brought two of her friends along. I went down on my knees and gave her a rose, and proposed her for marriage. She was shocked, and there was a strange but happy smile on her face. She couldn't decide how to react, so I asked her to answer me with a yes or no. She said, 'Yes, I accept your proposal.' Then I made a dance performance dedicated to her, and she was pleasantly surprised by it, as I had never danced before in the 14 years of my school life.

Our exams were approaching, so I stopped writing a letter to her, as it would disturb her. Soon the school would end. Class 12 examinations were about to start, and all I would worry was how would I be able to see her after the exams, and how would I listen to her voice, among many other things. But I had faith in my love, so I wasn't worried about it and thought we would end up together eventually. As our exams started, we would find some way to wish each other the best for the exams every day.

My last exam was on the 24th of March, and after that, we would barely get to meet. So I made a plan to meet her at school. After the exams were over, we returned to the school and would just look into each other's eyes. We had this strange feeling that we would never meet again. Don't know what came over both of us, and we hugged and started crying. It was the first time we hugged each other. She had tears in her eyes, and they were falling on my hands. I wished for everything to stop then and there. Again, I felt that we were seeing each other for the last time, and that everything would end soon.

In the end, she told me that she would try her best to make time for me, and then we hugged again and confessed our love to each other. We left for our homes shortly after.

Since I was in the science stream, my exams had ended but hers hadn't, as she was from the commerce stream and still had a few exams remaining. I would go to the school to wish her luck and would only get to see her then. Once our exams were over, both of us started looking for colleges for ourselves. She would talk to me on the phone when she could. I don't know how she would manage to talk to me, as it was difficult for her to do it. We would talk only once a week but would share everything. Things were going fine until then.

On the 24th of May, I went to meet her at her home after almost two months. I met her, and we hugged. Barely five minutes had passed when a relative of hers arrived and saw us together and told everything to her parents. I told her to put all the blame on me, but she said that she would not do anything like that and handle it. I told her that her future would be ruined if she wouldn't do that, but she didn't budge on her decision.

Her father came to our home to talk it out. He told my parents that I had threatened to kill everyone in her home if Kanika didn't agree to be in a relationship with me. My parents were shocked, but they knew I wouldn't say something like that, so they had my back. They said that it might be 99% my mistake but 1% hers too, and that I would never say something so brutal as her father claimed. So, I sorted everything out with her father.

About five days later, a friend of hers messaged me and said that I didn't do right by her and betrayed her, and that all guys are the same. I asked her exactly what I had done. She said that I had claimed I would take up the responsibility of everything that happened between Kanika and me, but when she tried to pin the blame on me, I changed my ways and that's how I betrayed her. She asked me to forget Kanika, and that she doesn't even want to hear my name. And I never was able to talk to her after that.

I just wanted to make things clear as to how exactly I betrayed her. I only wished for her happiness wherever she was. All I wanted was to never see tears in her eyes again. And if I could clear everything, I wouldn't even so much as peek in her direction anymore.

Soon after, I took admission in a BTech college and started living in a hostel. I would cry every day and wanted to know how and what I had done wrong. Every day I would think about ending my life, and often the idea of suicide crossed my mind. I had become a complete alcoholic by then, as I would lose my consciousness and would sleep.

Every morning, I would have a smiling face in front of everyone, but when alone in my room, I would sit quietly and beat myself up. I would wonder and ask myself in the mirror that why I did such stupid things, and if I wasn't worthy of love, why did I even bother. I told myself that I was guilty of making her cry so many times. I wouldn't do much but look at her photos and talk to her imaginary self. My friends would think I was going insane, as I would close my eyes whenever something was wrong and would talk to her.

Shortly after, on 11 October 2014, my school friend called me around 10 pm and asked if I wanted to speak to Kanika. I told him to stop mocking me; my fuse was already short lately and I wanted to have a drink, so he should stop bothering me, and I would talk to him the next morning.
Meanwhile, a voice said in the background, 'Hello, Kanika here.' She was on a conference call with us. For almost five minutes, I stopped in my tracks, took a deep breath, and said, 'Hello.'

She asked me how I was, what I was up to, and how my life was going. I told her that I was doing alright, and I had opted for a BTech course.
Then, I cut all formalities and asked her upfront why she had called me that day. She said that she felt like it, and asked if there was anything wrong in doing that. I was surprised to hear that. I asked her why the girl, who didn't want to hear my name, is calling me now. She said that she wanted to talk to me, so she called.

She asked me what was new in my life, and said that Mohit was telling her I wanted to clear something up with her. I asked her to drop the topic, as neither would she be able to clear things up now would I be able to listen to things. She insisted that I tell her. I asked her to explain how I had betrayed her then. She replied that it was all a misunderstanding, and her parents had convinced her that I wasn't on her side and was thinking only of myself. She said that this statement had become set in her mind, and she apologised for it. She had been unable to separate the right from wrong, and since I hadn't supported her, she felt angry and felt that way.

I told her that her simple misunderstanding had ruined my life. Every day I would cry and would ask myself the reason for my wrongdoings, wondering what I had done with her. And all she had to say was that it was a 'misunderstanding'. I told her that my life had come to a standstill.

She dropped the topic and asked me how my love life was going, and said that I would have gotten a girl by now. I told her that it's going alright, the only difference is that the girl doesn't respond to me, and only I do the talking.
She asked me if the girl was dumb. I told her that she wasn't dumb but just far away.

She said that she understood what I was trying to say and asked whom I was referring to. She requested me to forget her and move on with my life. I asked her if I had troubled her or tried to contact her, she denied. I asked if I knew where she was studying or if I ever appeared in front of her, and if I didn't do any of those things, then it was my choice to love whoever I want to. And I told her that she could neither steal my memories nor could she remove her presence from my heart, as she had no right to ask me to do that. She said that she didn't mean what I thought, but it was all wrong, and how long would I continue doing that. I said that it would last for as long as it must, and I would love her with my life, and if I was, it was more exciting to do it that way, falling and getting back up again in love, and remembering her. The voice that I longed for would appear in front of me just by closing my eyes, and I could see her then. And I would talk to her whenever I wanted to, and that I had no one else in my life except her, and she was with me even then.

Then, I asked how she was doing and what was going on in her life. She said that it was good as well, and her studies were also doing great. We had started talking at 10:11 pm, and by the time I noticed the time again, it had already been 12:13 am. I was outside the hostel, and I didn't feel like going inside. As I got to talk to her again, I didn't feel like doing anything else then.

The call dropped soon afterwards, and since it was a conference call, I didn't have a number to call her back, I didn't have it saved. She called me again and said that probably Mohit's phone balance had exhausted.

She asked me to understand and to focus on my career and my studies and forget about her. I told her not to repeat the same story over and over again, and that I would not bother her by calling or messaging. I would even delete her number, and all I wanted was to clear things up with her about the backstabbing, and it was done.

Apologising, she talked to me for a while, and then she said that she is going back home. It was almost 6 am, and I asked who was accompanying her, and she said, 'No one.' It was an indirect way of asking me to meet her. I told her to enjoy her holidays and asked her if I could come to meet her if she didn't have a problem with it. She said that it was my call, and she was cool with it.

So, I left by the first metro before 6 am, and since it was my first time traveling in one, I had no idea about which route to take. Somehow, I arrived where Kanika was. I was meeting her after almost four or five months and kept on staring at her once we met. My appearance had changed by that time, I had much longer hair, and I dressed differently, obviously looking like a spoiled college brat.

We exchanged pleasantries, and then we left for some other place. On the way, she asked what we should do, and I told her that my decision was the same and that I loved her. She said that it wasn't right, and I asked her to explain to me what was right then.

Again, she asked me to forget her. She asked me why I would try to remember her and why did I love her even now, after everything that had happened. I told her not to repeat the same story, and that I never contacted her and never bothered her. I loved her, and she should not have a problem with that.
She said that she does have a problem with it, and she still loves me the way she did back then, and she could not forget me. She would cry remembering me daily. And then, she said that our parents wouldn't agree, and we don't have a future together, and I should try to understand that.

I said that it shouldn't be a problem; we wouldn't say anything to each other and would keep on loving just the way we were.

She refused and said that she wanted to be with me, travel with me, and wanted to make memories worth remembering, as we had none. She wanted to fight with me, make up with me, and share a lot of things with me.
And then, we held our hands together and said together, 'I love you.'

After that, we both left for Greater Noida together, and then she went home. When she came back, I went to meet her on the same day.

Everything was back to normal, and things were back to how they were before, not in a day but a matter of a second. She had gone through a transformation herself, the way she spoke, and other things as well. Slowly, we were back to our habit of talking and meeting again, and we would meet at least twice a week for a movie or lunch.

Then, it was her birthday on the 3rd of November. She was going to leave in the morning for her home to attend a wedding. So, I sent a cake to her PG on the 2nd itself.

And at midnight, on the 2nd of November, I stood below her PG and gave her a flower. Her roommate helped me a lot in arranging everything. She had dropped a rope from the balcony, and I tied the flower to it, and she pulled it up. Kanika became sentimental when she saw the flower. I told her to go inside, and when she did, she saw her roommate had arranged the cake, etc., for her. I told her to enjoy it, and that we would talk again later.

I went to meet her again at 6 am the next day. She fed me cake with her own hands, and I hugged her and wished her happy birthday. She did not want to leave me and go, but her family members were about to come, so I left. That day, neither did I talk to her nor could I spend the day with her. I was feeling terrible for this reason, but I knew she felt worse than me. But we met after two days and spent a reasonable amount of time together. We used to meet at least once a week.

Then, it was my birthday, and she wished me at precisely midnight. I had to go home in the morning, but I came back in the evening and went to meet her at 4 pm. We both went to India Gate, as it was the best place to spend time together since no known person would have spotted us there. We sat holding each other's hands and kept looking at each other. She was looking stunning that day. She was looking straightforward.

She knew that I loved suits, so she had decided to wear a suit that day to make me happy. She did everything that day which would make me happy.

It was freezing that day, but she wanted to eat ice cream. She was like a child when asking for something. She had to be given what she wanted, whatever it might be. But she would always smile after she got what she wanted, and that was enough for me.

She caught a cold after eating ice cream in the extreme cold weather. We both started laughing, as I had told her that she would catch a cold, but she had said it wouldn't happen. But she did catch a cold. I dropped her home after that and came back to my hostel.

We would no longer fight. We did fight every day but hardly for 15 or 30 minutes because neither of us could stay angry at each other for longer than that. We always had a lot of fun whenever we met, but it was sad when we had to go back as neither of us felt like going back to our respective hostels.

I even got her to try alcohol and cigarettes, as she wanted to try them out at least once but in my presence. The day she got drunk, she almost killed me with her charm. She was talking just like a child as if she was eight years old. I don't remember everything she said in her drunken stupor, but I remember her hugging me and saying, 'I love you so much, Aman. Please never leave me. Always be with me. I am very drunk today, so please do not let go of my hand. Please hold me like this always.'

She was always like a kid, but when she got drunk, I was in trouble because she would be even more childish.

On 31 December, I was home so I could neither meet her nor could I celebrate the New Year's eve with her. That was the day she drank alcohol with her PG friends for the first time. She called me at night, and God knows what all she said. She kept repeating one thing at least ten times. To appease her, I also kept agreeing with her. She kept saying, 'No, it is like this,' or 'No, it's not like this; it's as it was,' etc. I don't remember what all she kept saying, but she was missing me. I went to meet her the next day. We both went to our favourite cafe to drink coffee.

Her exams were over, so she was going to go home on 16 January. I met her on the 7th, but when I went to drop her back, we could not take our eyes off each other. She kept looking for me in the metro, and I kept searching for her laughter. There was an unknown fear that day, an unknown feeling in my heart.

We kept talking after that as usual, and everything was fine. I was supposed to meet Kanika on the 12th. On 11 January, I called her in the evening, but she cut my call without receiving it. I called her at least five to six times for two hours, but she kept cutting my call. So, I called her roommate after that. Even she cut my call but managed to message me by telling me not to call or message Kanika as her parents had found out about us, and she was going to go home that very day. Her mother was packing all her things.

I did not believe her and said that I was not in the mood for jokes. I hadn't spoken to Kanika for a while and asked her roommate to let me talk to her. Then, the roommate sent me a picture of Kanika's mother packing all her belongings. I understood then that everything will end yet again. I could feel Kanika's pain.

That day, Kanika showed me how much she loved me. She told her father neither to go to my house nor to talk to me because I was not at fault. She told her father that she was the one who had called me first, and that I had never tried to contact her. Since that day, I was not able to talk to her.

Time went by, and I still did not have any contact with Kanika. One day, I received her call.

'Hello,' she said.

No matter how much time had passed without talking to her, but her one 'Hello' could make my heart skip a beat.

I said, 'Hello, how are you?'

She said, 'I've spoken to you now, so I'm fine.'

I asked her what had happened that day. She said that she did not want to talk about what has passed. She does not want to think of all that or be reminded of what happened. I could hear in her voice how happy she was talking to me, but I could also feel the sorrow of not being able to meet me.

She then told me that she goes to tuition at 6 pm and asked me to meet her the next day, as she wanted to give me a letter. I agreed to meet her the next day.

The next day, I went to meet her. She was looking so pretty that I did not pay attention to anything else other than her. I did not want to pay attention to anything else. She gave me the letter, and I left to read it. She had explained everything in the letter as to what had happened that day, and how she handled everything. She explained that her parents do not trust her to this day because of it.

The next day, I gave her a letter. I explained to her, in the letter, that our connection was that of the soul, and everything would turn out fine. We spoke through letters for eight to nine days. In one of the letters, she asked me to give her a mobile phone. I said that someone might catch it, but she said that she would take care of it and manage it. So, I gave her a mobile phone the next day. We started talking every day at 11 pm, or whenever she could find time, she would message me. I was afraid that someone might catch her talking on the phone and confiscate it, but she was managing everything just to talk to me.

Four months passed like this. Whenever I wanted to see her, she would go to the temple, and I would meet her there.

Her semester exams were coming close, and she was going to be in Delhi for the exams. We became happy that we would be able to meet and talk.

One day, she messaged me at 11:45 pm. We messaged for a while, and then I told her to sleep as she had an exam the next day, and she had to wake up early. She insisted that she didn't feel like sleeping and wanted to talk more. I agreed but said that we would talk only till 12. She agreed and said that we'd talk for only 15 minutes but on call.

Even I wanted to talk to her, so I told her to wait and called her. We had spoken for only 3 minutes 26 seconds when the call got disconnected. I thought someone might have come; that is why she cut the call. So I messaged her, but she did not reply for a very long time. Then I called her up, but her brother picked up the call, so I understood that we were caught again, and everything would be over. After some time, she messaged me that her brother Piyush caught her talking to me and read all the messages, and even her mother arrived just then. She did not know what would happen then because her mother and brother will tell her father in the morning. She said she might not even be able to give her exam.

I went to the crossroad near her house early in the morning to see whether she would go to give her exam or not. I saw her coming with her mother, so I understood that she was allowed to appear for the exam. Once her exam was over, she called me from the one of her friends' mobile phone. Right off the bat, I asked how her exam went. She said her exam went well. She asked me what we should do now, as her mother would tell her father everything once her exams are over.

I said that we have one month; we would think of something. Kanika asked me to give her another mobile phone, as she would not be able to talk to me otherwise, and we won't be able to come up with some plans as well. She said that we both would have to find a solution to this. I refused, but she kept insisting, so I gave her another mobile phone the next day. She kept it hidden. On the day of the next exam, even I went with her. We were both terrified, as we thought everything might end this time for good. But we were each other's strength, so we kept thinking of what to do. She was very depressed and used to talk like a madman, but as long as we were together, we were happy.

One day, she messaged me, 'Aman, please elope with me, and we will instead leave a body of my height and weight. I can't stay here anymore; it's driving me crazy. I am feeling suffocated inside the house. Neither my mother nor my brother is talking to me. It feels like I am in a stranger's house. I will stay anywhere with you.'

I knew this wasn't possible, so I tried to make her understand, but she refused to budge. She started behaving weirdly with me, thinking that I was trying to save myself. But the truth was that she was depressed and was feeling suffocated at home.

One day, her mother told her father everything, and her parents came to my house. It was to be decided that day what will be our fate. Her father put the phone I had given her in front of my father. And then, he said, 'Your prince son gave this to my daughter.' My father was looking at me with anger.

My father asked me, 'What do you want to do? You have destroyed our reputation. What do you want to do now?'

I said very softly, 'I want to be with her. I want to marry her.'

My father said, 'Alright, if that makes Aman happy, I am ready.'

Then, he asked Kanika what she wanted. I was looking at her, and she also agreed that she wanted to be with me and marry me. Then, she asked her father to say what he thought. He refused and said that he would not let Kanika marry me. My father asked why.

Her mother then said that she would end up staying here and going nowhere.

My father said, 'We will make a new house for them, wherever you want. Nothing is bigger than their happiness for me.'

But Kanika's father said that they did not consent to marriage at all, saying that I was the biggest thug of that area, I was rude, etc. Then, my mother got angry and said, 'Even we don't want the marriage,' and then took out all her anger on Kanika. She said a lot of things to her, which she should not have. At last, they were deciding what to do now. Then, the parents said that its better if everything ends between Kanika and me.

Then, I somehow gathered my strength and asked in front of everyone if I could talk to Kanika for two minutes alone. Both our parents agreed, so I took her to my room, and we were all alone. I could see that Kanika had tears in her eyes, but she was trying hard not to cry. I was crying because I felt like everything was being taken away from me.

Kanika said, 'Aman, we have to be strong. If you break, who will support me? You are my rock. You want me to be happy, right? Then please promise me that you will never cry again.'

I nodded to show my agreement. I requested that I did not want anything except that we talk three days in a year. Kanika agreed but asked which days. I said, '4 September, 3 November, and 24 November'. She agreed but asked me to stop crying and asked me to smile. She said that we have to make ourselves secure because we are each other's strength. She reminded me that I always tell her not to cry. She made me swear on her that I would not cry. I closed the door of the room and hugged her. She could not hold back anymore and started crying. We told that we loved each other, and then she left the room. I couldn't bear to watch her go, so I stayed back in the room.

One day, she messaged me from her friend's mobile phone. She told me that no one was talking to her at her home. Everyone was ignoring her. She told me everything that was happening with her. Then, she messaged me on 4 September. We talked for 10-15 minutes, then she left.

We were able to talk once or twice a week but only for five to ten minutes. Kanika's next message was on 13 October. She told me that she pierced her nose and sent me a picture. I complimented her, but I didn't think she was looking that good. Then, she reminded me what our parents told us – that we have to move on from each other. I said that I would not be able to move on, but she said that we would have to try and do it. Then, she messaged that she had to go home, so she said bye. I messaged her, 'Listen, I have to say one thing.' But she did not respond. I wanted to tell her that I will never be able to move on from her, and I knew that even she would not be able to move on from me, but she was gone by then.

I messaged her friend the next day to ask if she had come to meet her. But her friend replied that she had not. I kept messaging her the next day and the day after, but her response was the same, that Kanika had not come. 1 November arrived like this. I thought she would message me, but she didn't. On 3 November, I kept thinking about what gift to give her which would make her very happy. I wanted to give her the best gift I had ever given, which would make her very happy, and she would not feel that I am not with her. I thought I would tattoo her name. So, on 2 November, I went and got her name tattooed on my left hand. I celebrated her birthday with my friends at night. I knew she would message me. I did not sleep all night because I thought she could message me any time after midnight.

Until 8 am she had not messaged me. I messaged her friend to tell her to get Kanika to speak to me when she goes to her. She agreed and said that if Kanika came, she would get her to speak to me. I told Kanika's friend to call her. I was confident she would come. I messaged her again at noon to ask whether she talked to Kanika. Her friend said that there was some work at Kanika's house, so she might not come. I sent her the photo of my tattoo and told her to show to Kanika, as this was Kanika's birthday gift. I messaged six or seven of her friends asking the same thing, to talk to Kanika so that I could wish her. All of them replied the same thing, and if they called her, Kanika's mother might get suspicious. But one of her friends agreed to call her. When she asked Kanika to talk to me, Kanika refused and said she would not be able to talk to me. She even sent me a screenshot of the conversation. I thought Kanika must not be able to talk to me because of her family members.

My birthday was around the corner, so I thought she would message me. All of her friends wished me on my birthday, except her. I asked her friends if Kanika had asked them to wish me or if there was a message for me from her. Everyone said that they had not spoken to Kanika. I asked one of her friends if she could make me talk to Kanika just once somehow, or call Kanika to her house. She told me that Kanika did not want to talk to me anymore. She has moved on and that I should move on too. I still asked her if she could get me to talk to Kanika just once, but she couldn't.

I used to ask her friends daily if anyone had spoken to her, but everyone would respond the same that no one had talked to her. All her friends were irritated with me because I used to ask them every day if she had spoken to them. Then, I stopped asking them thinking that one day or the other she would talk to them, and I'll ask them then. And, I also thought that if I had made some mistake, I would say sorry to her. I knew she would forgive me because I was already being punished enough.

Time moved on rapidly. I did not know where Kanika was and what she was doing, except that she was pursuing an MBA. I used to check every single notification that would pop up on my phone and started receiving all the calls from unknown numbers hoping it would be her. Everything had changed. It felt like the only thing that remained was me waiting for her. I did not know how time went by. Months passed by while I waited for her call.

4 September came again, and I waited again. I asked her friends if she had messaged anything, or if she had come to meet them. All of them responded the same that she had not messaged them. I felt weird, but I dismissed it. I ordered lunch for myself, and then I purchased two tickets for a movie and went to watch it alone. I closed my eyes and pictured that moment when she told me on that very day that she only wanted to be with me. I was trying my best to divert my mind, but I was unable to do so.

Then, it was her birthday. This time I did not do anything. I just bought a cake and sat alone with it. I cut the cake at midnight, and I cried and cried. I wished her out loud and kept crying. I was missing her. So, I took out her photo and kept looking at it. I poured my heart out to her picture. I asked her questions, and I thought of answers. Then, I went home. I asked one of her friends if she wished Kanika and she said yes. I asked her to wish her on my behalf as well, but she did not reply. I didn't say anything as well and did not message her any further.

Then, my birthday arrived. I knew Kanika would not message me, but I still held out hope. But there was no message. That day, for the first time, I thought that maybe she has honestly forgotten me and has moved on. I held out hope that someday we would meet. I kept hoping that one day she would message me.

Meanwhile, I got busy with my business. Whenever I was alone, I used to remember my time with Kanika, and that's why I always tried to keep myself busy. I made myself so busy that I did not have time to think about myself or anything else.

Months had passed since I last saw her. I used to go to temples every day to pray that one day she would talk to me. I do not think any place of worship was left where I did not go to pray. I visited every temple, every mosque, every gurudwara to pray for her happiness. The person who would not set foot in any temple started visiting every place of worship.

11 October 2018 - Two years later

After two years, she messaged me on Instagram, 'Hello.'

I replied, 'Hello, how are you?'

She said that she was okay.

I asked her how was her hatred towards me lately. She responded it'd been the same for the last two years and asked me to tell her something else.

I told her that I had nothing to say, I was doing good, and I liked that she messaged me.

She said, 'I did not message to ask you how you were. I just wanted to say that you should move on. It is not that big of a deal to forget someone.'

I asked her if she had managed to forget me.

She said yes. She said that someone told her that I was still stuck in the past, and she thought it was her duty to tell me to move on, and there was no use of waiting for her. She wanted to say just this, and the rest, it was my life, and I was free to do whatever I wanted. She did not want to talk to me any further and asked me to delete the chat if I could.

I agreed. But I asked Kanika if I could wish her on the 3rd of November. She said that she would not reply to any messages. She said bye and said that she only wanted to tell me to move on in life.

I did not talk to her again and directly messaged her on her birthday at midnight. I also sent her a photo of the cake. She replied, 'Hmmm. Thank you.'

I did not message anything after that. I messaged in the morning, asking, 'Am I that bad a person that you have started hating me?'

She replied, 'I don't hate you, but I cannot tolerate all this anymore.'

I asked her if we could meet once. She said that it would not be possible, and that we will never meet again.

I requested her a lot, but she refused. She said that she had an exam and wanted to study. She told me to let her focus and not to message anymore.

I tried to find out where her exam was and found out it was somewhere in Noida. I looked in every college in Noida, where exams were ongoing but could not find any link. I made her swear on me and asked to meet only once. Maybe she respected my word and said that she would meet me after her exam. I was very excited to meet her. I got ready in the morning and left to meet her. I thought of so many things to tell her on my way to meet her.

She came to meet me after her exam, and I kept looking at her.

She said, 'Yes, tell me, what do you want to say? I don't have a lot of time, so please be quick.'

I said, 'Nothing, I just wanted to meet you. You can leave.'

She replied, 'Think properly, as it is the last time we meet, and we would never meet again. And I would not honour any kind of promises you invoke either.'

I said that I just wanted to see her because I had forgotten what I thought I would say. I asked her if things can be just the way they were before. She denied and said, 'Aman, it is not that difficult to forget someone. Please move on in your life, as I will never come back in yours.'

I asked her, 'What happened that you went so far away from me?'

'You know very well what happened. We promised our parents. And I bore a lot of difficulties, but I cannot anymore,' she said.

I said, 'All right. Tell me where to drop you.'

She asked me again if that's all I had to say because she would not be able to meet me again ever and won't even be able to talk on message, so if I had anything else to say, I should say it as it was the last time she would meet me.

I said, 'That's all I had to say. And about forgetting you, I don't think I can ever move on.'

She responded, 'Don't say that you don't want to move on. Aman, life is too long, and you have to move ahead in your life and be happy.'

I said, 'Why do you have a problem? It is my life, and I will live it how I want to. I want to live like this only. I feel like you're always with me. Whenever I have a problem, I close my eyes, and I find you with me. I don't want anything more than this.'

She asked me what I would feel if she did the same thing. I said that I would have felt horrible that because of me, someone would be spoiling their life.

She then said, 'Then why are you making me feel like that. Please move on. I cannot come back to you now because I gained back the trust of my family with a lot of difficulties. I cannot break their trust again.'

I asked her if I could drop her home. She refused. She said that I could drop her till the bus stop.

After gathering a lot of courage, I asked her if I could hold her hand. She stared at me for a while but kept quiet. I asked again, then she nodded. As soon as I held her hand, she closed her eyes. I felt like she stopped breathing for a while. Her eyes filled with tears, and she said very softly, 'I love you so much,' and started crying.

She kept crying and said, 'Why do you love me so much? Why don't you go away from my life? Leave me be. Even I feel like talking to you, spending time with you, fighting with you, making up with you. But then I remember the taunts of my family members, so I let things be as they are. Did you ever think about how I am without you? I think of you every single moment. I keep wondering how you must be without me and what do you do when you need me but I am not there. But I manage to hold myself together. But the truth remains that we can never be together. That is why, I want to go far away from you. I tried not to talk to you ever again, but that day I could not stop myself, and I messaged you.'

She kept talking, and I kept looking at her. I put my finger on her lips all of a sudden and said, 'See, we love each other, and that is enough for us.'

She cried and said, 'I love you, Aman. I cannot live without you. But now we will never meet or talk again.' And with that, she left.

The day our parents can understand our love is the day we will be together again. I am still waiting for her. There is a sort of thrill in all this waiting. It feels like I am in a different world where I can spend all my life with the only hope that, one day, we shall be together again.

Aman

'Main to bikta raha tere saher
Main kitabo ki tarah
Ek tujhe hi fursat na mili
Mujhe padhne ki.'

-Anonymous

Printed by Libri Plureos GmbH in Hamburg,
Germany